SESAME STREET

Bert and Ernie's Great Adventures

Waddle-Waddle Penguin

Adapted by Kathryn Knight from the script by Luis Santeiro

LEVEL **1** READER

READING LEVEL

Published by Dalmatian Press, LLC. All rights reserved.
Printed in Guangzhou, Guangdong, China.

The DALMATIAN PRESS name is a trademark of Dalmatian Publishing Group,
Franklin, Tennessee 37068-2068. 1-866-418-2572.

"Here we are!" said Ernie.
"It is a land of ice and snow."

"It is also a land of penguins,"
said Bert. "Look!"

Waddle-waddle-waddle.

"There is one now," said Bert.
"Follow that penguin!"

Waddle-waddle-waddle
went the penguin.
Waddle-waddle-waddle
went Bert and Ernie.

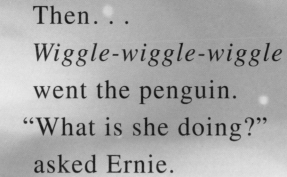

Then. . .
Wiggle-wiggle-wiggle
went the penguin.
"What is she doing?"
asked Ernie.

"She has an egg!" said Bert.
"She is a mama penguin."

The penguin grabbed Bert.
She sat him down on the egg.

"Hee hee hee," giggled Ernie.
"You are a papa penguin."

Splash!
The mama penguin
jumped into the water.
"Now what do we do?"
asked Bert.

SPLASH!

Splish!
The mama penguin popped up.
Splat!
She fed a fish to Bert.
"Mmmff!" said Bert.

Splash!
She jumped again.

"Brrr. It is very cold.
It is time to go home,"
said Ernie. "TAXI!"

"That is so silly," said Bert.
"There is no taxi here."

"Hee hee hee!" giggled Ernie.
"Our sled dog is named Taxi.
Come on, Bert. Let's go!"

"No!" said Bert. "I cannot go.
I need to stay on the egg.
Uh-oh. Where *is* the egg?"

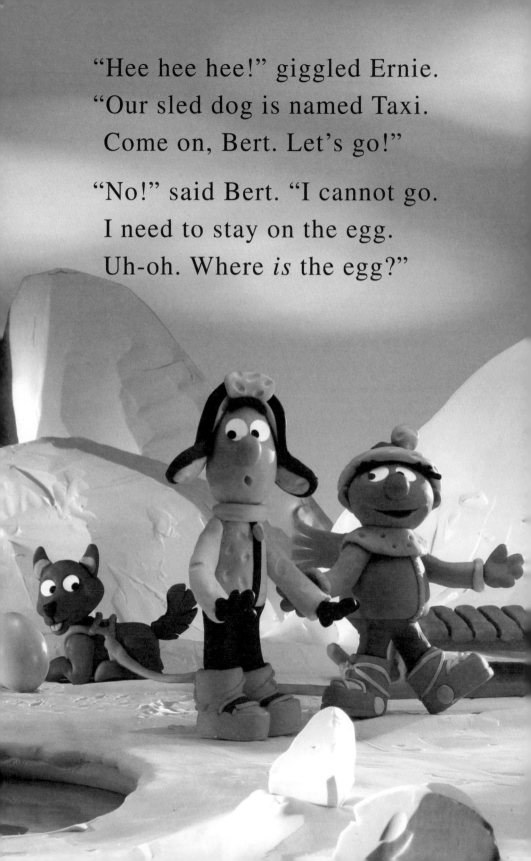

Oh, no!
Taxi had the egg.
Oops! He pushed it
down a snowy hill.

"Follow that egg!"
called Ernie.
Zoom!

Splash!
The mama penguin
popped up with a fish.
But where was her egg?
Where was papa Bert?
Waddle-waddle-waddle.
She went away to look.

Bert and Ernie found the egg.
Bert sat on the egg.
Ernie went to play.
"I hope the mama penguin
can find *us*," said Bert.

Ernie and Taxi
made snow angels.
"This is fun!" said Ernie.
"Arf-arf!" said Taxi.

"Bert!" called Ernie.
"Come play with us!
Bert? Where are you?"
Ernie looked.
He did not see the egg.
He did not see Bert.

"Help!" called Bert.
"I am out here!
The ice cracked!
I am going away
on the water!
Help! Help!"

"Oh, no!" said Ernie.
"How can I help you?"

Waddle-waddle-waddle.
The mama penguin found Ernie.
She looked for her egg.
She looked out at the water.
SQUAWK!!

"You can help," said Ernie.
Ernie got rope from the sled.
He put it on the penguin.
"Swim to your egg," he said.

The penguin swam to Bert.
Bert grabbed the rope.
The penguin pulled.
She swam and she pulled.
She pulled Bert and
the egg all the way back.

"Yay!" said Ernie.
Ernie hugged Bert.
Bert hugged Ernie.
He hugged the mama penguin.
"Thank you!" Bert said.
"But I am *not* a papa penguin."

"Look!" said Bert.

Wiggle-wiggle-wiggle
went the little egg.
Crack!
A baby penguin!

The mama penguin
hugged her little baby.
She let Bert hug her baby.

"Awwww. You are a
cute little baby," said Bert.
"You are—*mmmff!*"

Mama fed a fish to Bert.
"Hee hee hee!" giggled Ernie.
"She wants to thank you
because you were a good papa.
I hope you like fish, Bert!
Hee hee hee!"